How did humans and language originate?

Abdul Waheed

How did humans and language originate?

Abdul Waheed

notionpress

CERTIFICATE OF PUBLISHING

We're proud to present this certificate of publishing to

Abdul Waheed

for successfully publishing

HOW DID HUMANS AND LANGUAGE ORIGINATE?

on 28-12-2022

*"A writer's life and work are not a gift to mankind; **they're a necessity"** ~ Toni Morrison*

Surrender

This book is dedicated to the memory of my late father Haji Ubairdur Rahman (Munna Bhai) and younger brother Abdul Hameed. May Allah Taala (God) give peace to his soul.

Aamen.

Table of contents

Preface

How did man originate, this is a very complex and mysterious question which has been going on for centuries and its investigation is going on day by day. Similarly, there are many guesses about the language too, but it is not known, the search is going on continuously, but the proof of the script itself is found a little or possibly. Both these subjects are very interesting and mysterious. On the occasion of this, this book is presented in front of you, some of which has been revealed with some information. If you have more information than this, please inform,

Date - 23/12/2022

thanks,

Origin of Man

(According to Hinduism) -

Question) Has this world originated from God or from others?

(Answer) The instrumental cause has originated from the Supreme Soul, but its primary cause is nature.

(Question) Didn't God create nature? (not answer . He is eternal.

(Question) What is called eternal and how many substances are eternal?

(Answer) God, the soul and the cause of the world, these three are eternal.

(Question) What is the proof in this? (Answer) Dwa Suparna Sayuja Sakhaya Samanam Vriksha Pari Shaswajaate. Tayoranya: Pippalam svadvatpanashnannyo abhi chakshiti..1.

R 0 M 0 1. Su 0 164 m 0 20. शाष्टिथभ्यः समभ्यः ॥ Yaju : 0 a 0 40 m 0 8 ॥ (dwa) which both Brahman and Jiva (suparna) likeness of consciousness and sustenance qualities (sapuja) universally united (sakhaya) mutual friendship are eternal eternal and (samanam) like that (vriksham) tree with eternal root cause and branch form effect i.e. The one who becomes gross and disintegrates in annihilation is the third eternal substance. The qualities, actions and nature of all three are also eternal (tayoranyah). One type is the enjoyer and the second God is not the enjoyer of the fruits of actions (anashnan) but is shining everywhere, that is, inside and outside. Jiva to Ishwar, Ishwar to Jiva and Prakriti to both; All three are eternal. 1. (Shashwati 0) That is, God has made sense of all the knowledge through the Vedas for the eternal eternal living beings. (Question) – Was the human being created first or the earth etc.? (Answer) Earth etc. Because without the Earther, there can be no condition and upkeep of man.

(Question) Were one or many human beings created in the beginning of the world or what? (Answer) Many. Because the creatures whose deeds were to be born in the Aishwarya world, God gives them birth in the beginning of the world. Because man is a sage. Tato Manushya Ajayant It is written in Yajurveda. From this evidence it is certain that in the beginning many, that is, hundreds, thousands of human beings were born. And seeing in the world also it is certain that human beings are children of many parents.

(Question) In the beginning of creation, were human beings etc. created in childhood, youth or old age or in all three?

(Answer) Because the one who gives birth to children in youth, other human beings would be necessary for their upbringing and if he gives birth to children in old age, then Maithuni creation would not have happened. That's why it is created in youth.

(Question) Is there ever a beginning of the universe or not? (not answer . Just as night precedes day and day precedes night and night follows day and day follows night, so also doomsday before creation and creation before doomsday and doomsday behind creation and creation before doomsday; cycle from time immemorialLet's go It has no beginning or end, but just as the beginning and end of day or night are visible, in the same way the beginning and end of creation and holocaust keep happening. Because just as God, soul, the cause of the world are eternal in three forms, similarly the origin, condition and dissolution of the world are eternal in flow. Just like the flow of a river is visible in the same way, sometimes it dries up, sometimes it is not visible, then it is visible in the rainy season and it is not visible in summer. Such practices should be known as fluency. Just as God's qualities, actions, nature are eternal, in the same way the origin, condition, destruction of the world are also eternal. Just as there is no beginning and end to God's qualities, deeds, nature, similarly there is no beginning and end to his duties.

Reference- Satyarth Prakash, Maharishi Dayanand Saraswati.

The origin of human

is still an unsolved question that where did the origin of human begin, how did it happen, and how did it spread in the world? Who were its ancestors? Was man the same in the beginning as he is today? These questions are of equal importance to the origin of man for nonhuman beings as well. Cow, horse, elephant, pigeon, bat, snake, fish how, when and where were they born? We are humans, so we are more curious, disturbed and curious about every information related to humans. I originated from my parents, parents originated from their parents. Origin of his parents....? This statement (answer) is infinite, never ending. Nevertheless, a solid solution can be found by scientific discussion. Till now it was taught in biology that thousands of years ago modern man was not like today. It gradually evolved from other mammals that walked on two or four legs with physical changes through mutations over millions of years. Now the question is that a man must have at least one parent. should not be, because any living being is born from its parents and physical and mental,

are identical in quality. This means that due to the change of qualities in millions of years, our ancestors definitely cannot be like us. At the time of creation, Brahma created men and women (male and female) from Yogmaya by rubbing their thighs, due to which the progeny of human beings increased and expanded in India. Brahma, the Vedic and Puranic man did not know about the whole world, so the projected ideology of India came to a standstill. While the scientists of Europe believe that the first man was only 9000 years ago. On the other hand, Brahma created daughters Savitri and Saraswati and forcefully made them wives and increased the progeny of human beings and Hindus considered them as Adipurush. If not shooting arrows in the dark, what else is it? **Hindu mythology** is of the opinion that in every 71st Satyuga, the earth is submerged in which some humans survive on the Himalayas, due to which the population increases due to the birth of humans. Secondly, thousands of people go into hibernation in the valleys, which after thousands of years become alive in the same condition. Aryasamaji also claims that man as he is today, has been like this since the beginning and will remain like this till the end. It means that there is no physical and mental development of man, which is wrong on the principles of science. Vedic,

Hinduism and Arya Samaj shoot arrows in the dark. But this does not prove thatHe was the Adimata-Adipita (first man) of the scattered man in the world, whereas it has become clear from the DNA test that Arya (Brahmin) had come to India from Eurasia, then the theory of 71st Yuga or being buried in the Himalayas would have become invalid. Is . Spaniard Moses de Leon writes in his book "The Book of Splendor" in the 13th century that Jehovah created at the same time an "Adam" and a woman "Lilith" to become husband and wife. The reason she left Adam and went away. When Adam prays to God, then he creates Eve and provides it as a wife and orders that you increase the human population on earth.

According to the Bible, 2 lakh 9 Thousand years ago, Jesus had sent Adam-Eve to the earth as a punishment, from whom man originated and spread in every region. Jesus was in Jerusalem, so there were Adam-Eve, the progenitors of man. There should have been the culture and language of Jerusalem in the world, which is not there. Secondly, Christian Christopher Columbus of Italy came to India at the end of 14th century, after that Christians started coming to India, but not their ancestors. Today there are more than 10 million Christians. are in India, neither did they give up their culture, nor Indian cultureNeither adopted, nor imposed their culture on Indians, all Hindus converted to Christianity, who have no relation with their ancestors. Similarly, Muslims brought their own culture, which neither Tyagi nor Indian culture adopted. It is clear from this that people of every civilization of the world remained independent in themselves and were also successful in maintaining their identity. Therefore, the ancestors of all the humans of the world are not the same and modern humans did not originate at one place. Shooting arrows in the dark does not change scientific truth. 2 lakh 9 thousand years before the origin or development of Christian Islam religion 1400 years ago Who is the eyewitness of the story of Adam + Eve - Jew, Jehovah, Jesus or any prophet? nobody . There is no one among the Hindus who can prove the details of the period of Brahma-Saraswati/Savitri or Shiva. Everyone shoots arrows in the dark. It is about that man who was born first on earth and through whom he spread all over the earth. A creature produces a creature (child) like itself, what to talk about a lion with a pigeon, even a crow cannot be born in birds, a cat cannot be born from a cheetah, a rat cannot be born from a rabbit. Then of course man was born only from man. But the first man must also have been born from a man! This is not true, becauseToday's every creature was born from its respective ancestors and in many millions of years being affected by mutation, it got transformed into different creatures. This proves that human beings may not have originated from one parent at one place, because different species of human beings like Negro, Dravidian, Bhil, Anglo-Indian, Red-Indian, Japanese, Chinese, African, Tribal and Orangutan lived at their respective places. They kept getting transformed from their ancestors. All the civilizations in the world are only 9-10 thousand years old, in which time and civilization have been estimated by identifying houses, clothes, utensils, weapons, social structure etc. made by humans. We assume that we are descendants of fossil humans found in local civilizations, this does not prove that they were the first humans, because then again not in one place, people of civilizations discovered in every country or every continent or plot First there were humans. The question is where in the world was the first man born? This conclusion cannot be reached even from civilizations, because human beings of European civilization could not have come to Harappan civilization 10-15 million years ago, then without being uncivilized, scientific thinking and resourcefulness, they would not have been thousands of miles away. could go . For this we have to rely on the research of biology.

Creation place of human:

1. According to linguists like Max Muller, the creation place of primitive man is Central Asia.

2. Famous Bengali scholar Babu Umesh Chandra 'Vidyaratna' describes Mongolia in the book "Manavre Adi Janmabhoomi".

3. Swami Dayanand Saraswati Arya described Aryavarta (Tibet and the lower part of the Himalayas) in Satyarth Prakash.

4. In the Shatapatha Brahmana "Teshan Kurukshetre Dev Yajanam Aas Tasmadahu: Kurukshetram Devanan Dev Yajanam" The ancient gods used to perform Yagya in Kurukshetra, and they were born there, therefore they are the original humans.

5. According to the Bible and the Qur'an,--

the original birthplace of man is the "Garden of Eden" (the land of the monkeys). God made an effigy like himself in the garden on the fourth heaven (heaven), "Adam", breathed into his ear and left him alive. While roaming around, he fell asleep, took out his rib and created the woman "Hava". Out of jealousy of their love, the devil persuaded Eve to pluck and eat the fruit of the forbidden tree. Both of them did the same, which angered God. Throwing them on the earth, orders to create human progeny, from whom the human species was established in the world.

Tafsir of holy Quran

Tafsir ibne kathir
Surah Al Araf 7, ayat 11
Prostration of the Angels to Adam and Shaytan's Arrogance

Allah informs the Children of Adam about the honor of their father and the enmity of Shaytan, who still has envy for them and for their father Adam. So they should beware of him and not follow in his footsteps.

Allah said,

وَلَقَدْ خَلَقْنَاكُمْ ثُمَّ صَوَّرْنَاكُمْ ثُمَّ قُلْنَا لِلْمَلِيِكَة اسْجُدُواْ لاَدَمَ فَسَجَدُواْ

And surely, We created you and then gave you shape; then We told the angels, "Prostrate yourselves to Adam," and they prostrated,

This is like His saying,

وَإِذْ قَالَ رَبُّكَ لِلْمَلِيِكَة إِنِّى خَـٰلِقٌ بَشَرًا مِّن صَلْصَـٰلٍ مِّنْ حَمَإٍ مَّسْنُونٍ

فَإِذَا سَوَّيْتُهُ وَنَفَخْتُ فِيهِ مِن رُّوحِى فَقَعُواْ لَهُ سَـجِدِينَ

And (remember) when your Lord said to the angels:"I am going to create a man from dried (sounding) clay of altered mud. So, when I have fashioned him completely and breathed into him the soul (which I created for him), then fall (you) down prostrating yourselves unto him." (15:28-29)

After Allah created Adam with His Hands from dried clay of altered mud and made him in the shape of a human being, He blew life into him and ordered the angels to prostrate before him, honoring Allah's glory and magnificence. The angels all heard, obeyed and prostrated, but Iblis did not prostrate.

إِلاَّ إِبْلِيسَ لَمْ يَكُن مِّنَ السَّاجِدِينَ

except Iblis (Shaytan), he refused to be of those who prostrated.

We explained this subject in the beginning of Surah Al-Baqarah. Therefore, the Ayah (7:11) refers to Adam, although Allah used the plural in this case, because Adam is the father of all mankind.

Similarly, Allah said to the Children of Israel who lived during the time of the Prophet,

وَظَلَّلْنَا عَلَيْكُمُ الْغَمَامَ وَأَنزَلْنَا عَلَيْكُمُ الْمَنَّ وَالسَّلْوَى

And We shaded you with clouds and sent down on you manna and the quail, (2:57)

This refers to their forefathers who lived during the time of Moses. But, since that was a favor given to the forefathers, and they are their very source, then the offspring have also been favored by it. This is not the case in:

وَلَقَدْ خَلَقْنَا الإِنْسَـنَ مِن سُلَـلَةٍ مِّن طِينٍ

And indeed We created man out of an extract of clay (water and earth). (23:12)

For this merely means that Adam was created from clay. His children were created from Nutfah (mixed male and female sexual discharge).

This last Ayah is thus talking about the origin of mankind, not that they were all created from clay, and Allah knows best

Aasr al-Tafsir of the words of the Most High/Abu Bakr al-Jaza'iri

7 Al-A'raf , ayat 11

Abu Bakr Al-Jazairi (b. 1921 AD)

Interpretation of Aasr al-Tafsir of the words of the Most High/Abu Bakr al-Jaza'iri (d. 1921 AD),

words explanation:

We created you and then formed you: that is, We created your father Adam, that is, we formed him from clay and then shaped him into the noble human image that his children inherited after him until the end of human existence.

So they prostrated: that is, a prostration in greeting to Adam, peace be upon him.

Satan: The father of the devils from among the jinn, and his nickname is Abu Murrah, and he is the accursed Satan.

So descend from it: that is, from Paradise.

From the small: plural of small, humiliated, humiliated.

Because you misled me: that is, because you misled me.

reprehensible and repelled: abhorrent, reprehensible, and expelled.

Meaning of the verses:

The context continues to enumerate the blessings that God Almighty has bestowed upon His servants, which necessitate gratitude to Him, the Almighty, through faith in Him and obedience to Him. The Almighty said: {And We created you, then formed you} meaning, We created your father Adam from clay, then formed him with the human image that his children inherited from him, {Then We said to the angels: "Grandfather to Adam" and in this Another blessing is honoring your father Adam by commanding the angels to prostrate to him as a greeting and veneration for him. } That is, anything that made you not prostrate. Satan replied, saying :{I am.

[Al-Hijr: 38] And it is the annihilation of this world only, and that is before the resurrection. This answer came in Surat Al-Hijr, and here it said: "Indeed, you are of those who give the second thought." And Satan's intention in the respite is to be able to corrupt the largest number of the sons of Adam as revenge on them, since Adam was the reason for his expulsion from mercy. And when the Lord answered his request, He said: "Because You have misled me," meaning, You have led me astray, "I will surely follow for them Your straight path," meaning Adam and his descendants. What is meant by the path is Islam, since it is the straight path that leads the one who takes it to the pleasure of God Almighty. "Then I will certainly come to them from before them and behind them and on their right and on the Their left ones} He wants to surround them and prevent them from taking the straight path so that they will not be saved and perish as he perished, may God increase his destruction, and His saying: "And you will not find most of them thankful" This is Satan's saying to the Lord Almighty, and you will not find most of the children of Adam, because of whom you led me astray, grateful to you through faith, monotheism, and obedience.

And here God repeated his command to expel the accursed one, saying, "Come out of it," that is, from Paradise, "reprehensible and repelled," that is, abhorrent, expelled. "For whoever of them follows you, I will certainly fill Hell with all of you," meaning.

7 Al-A'raf , ayat 189

Abu Bakr Al-Jazairi (b. 1921 AD)

Interpretation of Aasr al-Tafsir of the words of the Most High/Abu Bakr al-Jaza'iri (d. 1921 AD), words explanation:

From one soul: the soul of Adam, peace be upon him.

And He made her husband from her: that is, He created her husband from her, and she is Eve. He created her from Adam's left rib.

To feel comfortable with her: that is, to become familiar with her and feel comfortable with her because she is of his gender.

When he had intercourse with her: that is, he had intercourse with her.

So she passed by it: that is, she was going and coming to fulfill her needs because of the lightness of pregnancy in the first months.

When she became heavy: that is, the burden became heavy in her stomach.

If you give us a good child, that is, a good child, not an animal but a human being.

They made him partners: that is, they named him Abdul Harith, and he is the servant of God Almighty.

So God is exalted above what they associate with Him: that is, the people of Mecca, as they associated idols in worshiping God.

And if you call them to guidance, that is, idols, they will not follow you.

Meaning of the verses:
God Almighty says to those who ask about the Hour due to the stubbornness and arrogance of the polytheists. He, that is, God {Who created you from a single soul and

made from it its mate} is the God worthy of worship, not idols and fetishes. For the Creator of you from a single soul, which is Adam, and from it He created Eve, He is worthy of deification and worship. Without any other of his creation. And his saying, "that he might be at ease with her" is a reason for his character, as he married her to her, since if she were of another gender, there would not have been intimacy and affection between them. And his saying, "when he had intercourse with her," meaning to have intercourse with her, "she carried a light load and passed with it," because of his fear, "and when it became heavy," meaning the burden burdened her, {d. Help God} that is Adam and Eve asked their Lord, the Almighty, saying, "If you give us a righteous person," meaning a righteous boy, "we will surely be thankful," meaning, to you. And the Almighty God responded to them and gave them good deeds. And God Almighty said: "And when He gave them good, they made for Him partners in what He had given them," where Eve named him Abd al-Harith, deceitfully from Satan, when he suggested this name to them, and it is from the hidden polytheism that is forgiven, such as if it were not for the doctor, so-and-so would have perished, and His saying: "So exalted is God above what they associate with Him." } return.

The criteria for existence of primitive man in the Himalayas:

1. The Himalayas are the highest and oldest mountain range in the world. 2. Due to being high when the earth is submerged, the Himalayas are the only possibility for human survival and regeneration.

3. Due to the first cooling of the hot earth on the Himalayas, there was a possibility of availability of suitable climate and food for human life.

4. The temperate climate is most suitable for the human progeny which must have been born first on the Himalayas. 5. The original humans still live here as evidence. 6. Conditions for growth and expansion of all colors are available on the Himalayas.

7. It is clear from the literature of Indo-Aryans and Iranians that man originated in the Himalayan region only, because this region is known to humans of every species of the world.

8. The whole world agrees with the concept of the origin of primitive man on the Himalayas.

9. David writes in the book "Harmonia" that the Himalayas are the highest, which is called 'Meru' mountain in Sanskrit. Meru is called by the Iranian people Mauru, the Greek Meros, the southern Turkish Meruva, the Egyptian Merai and the Assyrian Morakh.

10. Devika Paschime Parshwe Manasam Siddhasevitam in Shatpath Brahmin, Tadappedutrach Grihe Manoravasarparnam. That is, in the Himalayas, in a place called Manas, the original creation of man took place. There is Manas lake on the western side of the exit of Devika river, this name is due to the immortal creation.

11. The immersion of Manu took place on the Himalayas only.

12. In the Mahabharata, "Asmin himvatah shringe nasvam badhnetam achare" means Manu had quickly tied a floating boat in the event of a holocaust.

13. Vishwakarma also made planes and boats etc. during this period. 14. Charak context in Ayurveda In "Rishaya Khalu: Perhaps Kshatrina Pranavarashcha", it seems that sages used to live on the Himalayas only, who had come to South India through the route of Haridwar.

15. Scholars of Germany, Germany and Russia tell the birthplace of Aryans. European Central Asia and Lokmanya Tilak North Pole, Persian tells Iran. Nana Pavji has written in 'Aryavartantil Aryachi Janmabhoomi' that the Himalayas is the primordial birthplace of the Aryan gods.

Fossils:

Most of the fossils of early humans have been found in the world in a safe condition in the Rift Valley of East Africa. This valley crosses the borders of Ethiopia, Kenya and Tanzania. The study of fossils obtained showed that the human race originated at least 2.5 million years ago. The ancestors of human race or apes (ape) had originated from them 25-30 million years ago (50-60 million years ago, while modern humans originated only 2-3 million years ago. The father of A. has been recognized. Available evidence has shown that the aphorensis species of Australopithecus existed in the Rift Valley of East Africa 40 million years ago. There are 3 differences between the two - the brain of Australopithecus is smaller than that of apes and that of Homo is wider. The teeth were big chewers) and Homo's teeth were small (used to take modified foods), first used to walk and climb trees, Homo used to walk only on two legs. Homo hannilus, Homo rudolfensis and Homo ergaster have been known about 15-20 million years ago. For the emergence of new genera and species, genetic variation is required, which is produced by mutation and recombination. From among them, nature then selects the most successful genetic variants. In this way new dynasties are formed from old dynasties and theirNew species emerge. Homo erectus and then Homo sapiens were believed to have evolved from Homo ergaster in climate change. Homo erectus fossils are spread all over the world apart from Africa. **Modern humans (Homo sapiens)** probably evolved in Africa 2 million years ago and spread throughout the world. The study of the DNA of the mitochondria of human cells showed that 2 million years ago on African land, a woman developed mitochondria of modern DNA, which was more efficient than the mitochondria of earlier humans and passed on from her offspring to her descendants. kept reaching in and the adaptability was high. Still, there is a difference of opinion whether Homo sapiens was spread from Africa or evolved in many places in the world.

Almost 25 thousand years ago, a species of human, Homo neandertheensis, became extinct. The tools of the Middle Stone Age are the work of this man, and the development of Neanderthal and modern species is considered to be from the same species of Pithecanthopine human (Homo erectus). The earliest member of the human family is considered to be the Australopithecine human, from which the Pithecanthopine human evolved. In the opinion of anthropologist Dart, this primitive man lived without the use of bones, teeth and horns of other animals.

Used only as tools of transformation. Along with the fossils of Australopithecus human, many fossils of baboon monkeys and antelope deer were found in a cave. Both animals had marks of injuries on their heads etc. which were made on the living, such marks are not made in fossils. Although humans living in Levantine had used wheat and barley as food grains 12 thousand years ago, but humans living in Africa did not have knowledge of these food grains. About 10,000 to 12,000 years ago, some communities of humans started using wheat, barley, peas and lentils in food. Near the village "Bori" on the banks of Kukdi river, 100 km away from Poona, the white soil "Trefa" that came out of the volcano was found, on which ancient stone weapons were found. Beneath the ash there is red soil up to 6-8 meters below which human weapons were found. Volcanic ash contains potassium. Some potassium is radioactive which is converted into argon gas after a specified period of time. At the time of explosion, this light gas goes into the atmosphere. So at this time there is argon in the ash. That's why the amount of potassium and argon are compared for the age of ash. That ash of Bori village was estimated to be 14 lakh years old. comparativeIt has been found from the study that the properties of the ash of "Toba" volcano located in Sumatra are similar to the properties of this ash, while there is a distance of 2000 km between the two. According to the magnetic study of the black and red soils of Bori, their age is 7 lakh years. The time of ash shower in the sack is called 'Acheulean'. Human remains of this period have been found in Africa. On the basis of bones, he was called Homo erectus. Charles Robert's conclusion was that in nature a species of organisms is produced only once in a particular area. As their population increases, their territorial expansion goes on. After reaching different regions, changes in their characteristics begin to occur in new geographical conditions, due to which new species are formed. Under the influence of Thomas Malthus's theory of population, Darwin (1842) determined the theory of Natural Selection. Organisms struggle with each other to meet their needs, which lasts from embryo to lifelong. This is called struggle for life. The struggle for life helps nature to select such members of a species who are stronger, fitter and more tolerant than other members of the same species. Thus the natural selection of speciesit happens . Darwin showed it to his friend botanist Joseph Dalton Hooker after writing it in detail. Darwin was surprised when he read Alfred Russel Wallace's Natural Scientific Article on 18.06.1858. But together with him, a joint research paper of Darwin and Wallace was read on 01.07.1858 in the Linnaeus Society of London. Then on 24.11.1859, because of the book published in the name of 'On the Origin of Species by Means of Natural Selection Darwin', the religious people called Darwin an atheist, yet the second book 'The Variation of Animals and Plants under Domestication in 1868 and the third book' The Descent of Man and Selection in Relation to Sex was published in 1871 and was largely appreciated by the educated class. About 60 million years ago, the modern Cenozoic era began, in which nature paid special attention to mammals, which were successful. These were animals of the primate class. Man is also a well-developed creature of this class. Nature left the human Homo sapiens rich in intelligence and skills in an underdeveloped form about one lakh years ago, which has gradually attained this modern state.

The evolution of any creature (Evolution- Evolutionary Development) teaches us that humans have evolved from small and simple creatures (mammals like ape, chimpanzee, gorilla, gibbon, etc.) gradually by mutation over many millions of years. Therefore, man is not more than the best and supreme being. If the modern development of man had happened from these animals, then today these animals having some similarities would not have remained animals, all humans would have gone. This means that these creatures cannot be the ancestors of humans. The way the earth has been able to develop slowly over millions of years from a hot body of the sun to today's stage or the stage of emergence of organic wealth, it was not like this from the beginning. To know this clearly, "Oparin Theory" has to be understood.

Oparin Theory (Abridged): Russian scientist Alexander Ivanovich Oparin had propounded the first theory of the origin of life from non-living substances in 1924 under the name "Origin of Life". Oparin told the truth of Louis Pasteur's statement "The origin of the organism is from the organism itself" and said that life has developed only from the complex combination of chemical substances. The presence of methane on various celestial bodies is an indication that the early atmosphere of the earth was composed of methane, ammonia, hydrogenAnd being made of water vapour, it must have been highly reducing. The compounds formed by the combination of these elements would have further combined to form more complex compounds. The new properties resulting from the different configurations of these complex compounds may have laid the foundation for the regularity of life. Biological traits once started must have created the present living creation by walking on the path of competition and struggle. The hot earth became cold. Organic and inorganic salts, mineral elements were collected from the vapors of rainwater in the low-lying places (current sea). Organic compounds like ethane, methane, butone, ethylene, acetylene were formed, whose mutual reaction resulted in methyl alcohol, ethyl alcohol, oxy-hydro compound. Complex organic compounds were formed by the combined reaction of ammonia and water.In course of time, due to ultraviolet rays (X-rays/thundervolt) all the sugars became glycerine, fats, acids, amino acids, lactic acid, pyrimidines, pyrenes which are the main factors of life. Now nucleorides - RNA and DNA (active as hormones) became liquids which were self-energetic. Haldane (1920) called it Probiotic soup. Because of these, proteins and nucleic Acids are formed, which lead to the formation of nucleoproteins.

Started Cell wall was formed for the first time for organisms due to which division of nucleus was possible. Now tissues started being formed by similar compounds for a similar function. A cell wall was formed to filter the cytoplasm. In course of time, they became self-sufficient creatures who started preparing and digesting their own food. Some cells started manufacturing food and green material (chlorophyll) in the presence of sunlight and the development of vegetation (trees and plants) started. The origin and development of living beings started from this stage. Now the cells independently formed the autotrophic nucleus, mitochondria, chloroplast, Golgi complex, lymosomes, etc. and in this way the evolution of single-celled animals (animals) became possible parallel to vegetation, like Paramecium and Amoeba. In order to live in the environment of the earth and in the strange conditions of each other, the living beings started life struggle. First one-celled (amoeba, paramecium) organisms were formed, from which fish etc. originated in millions of years. Spine animals evolved from invertebrates which are divided into groups like fish, birds, reptiles, mammals, rodents, amphibiansEtcetera . Mammals include wild animals such as lion, leopard, leopard, wolf, cat, dog, camel, elephant, cow, buffalo, human etc. It is certain that all these have evolved initially from a common ancestor over millions of years. All birds must have had an ancestor. Similarly, the second group of mammals, cow, buffalo, horse, donkey, goat, monkey, bear, chimpanzee, gorilla, orangutan, etc. must have had the same ancestors, from which new and modern creatures must have developed due to transformation in millions of years, in which one He is human. It was not the same with modern man etc. because it was different from the study of fossils. With time he developed his body, needs, housing, food, means of travel and security and became a modern man. By crossing the stone, copper, silver-gold, machine, weapon-weapon era from modern human animal, it became modern civilized, beautiful, educated, scientific and knowledgeable-meditator. From this we cannot prove that man was born from one place and spread all over the world, because if the man of the world was born at one place, he would have been of one kind, not different like Negro, Japanese, Anglo-Indian, Dravidian. , Red Indian etc.

Conclusion:

If humans evolved from monkeys, then today's monkeys should have been humans, monkeys should not have existed today. Had humans evolved from chimpanzees, gorillas, orangutans, gibbons, orangutans, or orangutans, these creatures would not exist today, because they would have evolved into humans sometime in the past. Now it is clear that whatever man has evolved from, that creature must have remained just like man, but undeveloped, uncivilized, anti-social, uneducated, non-linguistic and incomplete. Since there are many species and languages of man in the world, therefore man cannot keep the place of origin in one region at a time. It has evolved from its own ancestors on different terrains. That's why many species of humans (Homo Homo) continued to develop in many places.

World famous myth

Myths of Babylon

Creation of the World- After defeating the enemy, Mardak got busy in the creation of the universe. Standing at Tiamat's feet, he crushed Tiamat's skull and tore Tiamat's body in half. He created the sky from the upper half and the earth from the lower half. He made a mountain by setting Tiamat's head on the earth and from her eyes flowed the two rivers of Mesopotamia, Tigris and Euphrates. Marduk appointed his grandfather Anu, the father of heaven, Eya of the earth and Enlil of the wind that flows between earth and sky. He created Sin i.e. Moon and entrusted him with the responsibility of illuminating the night and gave the task of spreading light during the day to Shams i.e. Surya, the son of Sin. After this, he made the earth strong and built a huge temple on it, so that the gods coming on the journey of the earth can stay in it and they can be respected. Marduk announced that the rent for the temple built by him,

The name Babylon means 'the house of the great gods'. The protection of the temple was entrusted to Eya. Now the problem arose that who would offer bhog to the deities and who would serve them? To solve this problem, Marduk announced that he would collect the blood and bones from which he would create a wild creature and name it Man. The aim of human life should be to serve the gods. On the orders of Eya, it was decided that after killing the deity who provoked Tiamat, humans would be created from his blood. The assembly unanimously declared that it was King who had instigated the rebellion. They tied up the king and presented him before Marduk and Eya. Iya killed the king and created humans from his blood. After this Iya told the humans that the purpose of their life was to serve the gods. The deities spent the next two years building the temple. When the temple was built, it was dedicated to Marduk. The dedication ceremony went on for several days and finally Marduk was declared emperor of Babylon forever. Cataclysm - In Babylonian myths, a detailed description of the cataclysm i.e. the devastating flood caused by angry gods on the land and people of Sumer and Babylonia is found.

The Holocaust saga was first written down in 2100 BCGiven . In the Marduk myth it is indicated that the gods created mankind to serve them. So when he saw that humans had become indifferent towards performing their duties towards the gods, his anger towards mankind and his decision to destroy it was very natural, but the gods who created mankind with their own hands , They instinctively started treating and loving them like their own children. That's why they were not ready that the creation created by them should be completely destroyed. The myth is described as follows: "Shurappaka, an ancient city on the banks of the Euphrates River, was the capital of Sumer. Both gods and humans lived in the city, gods in their temples and humans in their homes when humans and gods grew old. , then Enlil, the ruler of the gods, called a meeting of the assembly of the gods and complained to the gods that the number of human beings living on the earth had increased beyond counting and that they were making a lot of noise. The noise is like that of a herd of wild buffaloes. The commotion and running of men has given me sleepless nights." Enlil's complaint against humans was similar to that of Tiamat's against her children. Enlil, like Apsu, determined that sheWill destroy the human race completely and for this purpose, he ordered Adag, the god of rain, to rain torrential water on the earth day and night and continue this process until the whole earth including the mountains is submerged in water. He also told Adag that this cataclysm should be sent silently like a thief on earth, who would take away the food from the inhabitants of Shuruppaka and drown them to death. Enlil's proposal put before the assembly was supported by the goddess Ishtar and all other gods except Eya agreed with this proposal. Eeya sat silently thinking that he did not want to completely destroy the universe which he had painstakingly created with his own hands. Eya had a deep love for the human race, so he devised a plan to protect the seed of life on earth. By his divine powers he appeared before Uttanapiritham, the king of Shuruppaka and said to him, "You stand in your reed hut near the wall and listen to me. Faithfully and obediently." Utnapishtim stood by the reed wall and listened to Eya's voice. Eya said, "Shuruppak is soon going to be inundated in a great flood, so that it will be completely destroyed."

will go . Enlil has given this order with the consent of the gods. Iya told Utnapishtim to protect his life and he also suggested its way. He told the king that "uproot your house and make a huge boat shaped like a manjusha from its wood, whose length and width are the same." . This boat should be made of solid timber, so that Shams i.e. the rays of the sun cannot enter it. Apart from this, its holes and cracks should be filled so well that water cannot enter the boat through them. Eya said to Utnapishtim that "You take your wife, your relatives, artisans of F city, all kinds of grains, couples of all living things, animals and birds and get on the boat and when you get my signal, its door will be completely closed." Get it done On the request of the king, Eya also drew a sketch of the boat on the ground. Hearing this, the king asked the deity Eya, "When the people of Sharuppak will ask me what I am doing, what will I answer?" Eya replied, "Tell them that I have learned that Enlil hates me so much that I can no longer stay in your city, so much so that I cannot set foot anywhere in the kingdom of the god Enlil." . So I will go to the deep sea and live with my lord Eya. But I also learned thatGod Enlil is about to shower prosperity on you. One evening after a storm you will find extraordinary birds and fish and your land will grow rich crops. "The artisans of Shurappaka took five days to prepare the huge boat of Utnapishtim. It was 200 feet long, 200 feet wide and 200 feet high and had about an acre of space inside it. Inside the boat, the king prepared a seven-storey wooden building. and divided each storey into nine sections. On the sixth day every hole and crack in the boat was carefully sealed and on the seventh day it was lowered into the waters of the Euphrates River. He boarded the boat carrying a pair of grass and grain. As soon as the god Adaga covered the sky with fierce storm clouds, the king closed the door of the boat at the signal of Shams. Left to wander at the mercy of the raging storm. The whole creation was plunged into darkness and the rising waters flooded and destroyed the people of Shuruppak and all the living beings. When Goddess Ishtar saw this scene of apocalypse on earth, she Screamed and he started regretting that the creation he himself had created and lived But he had immense love for him, why did he support Enlil when he proposed his destruction?

This remorse was not only in Ishtar's mind. Seeing the enormity of the destruction, all the gods except Enlil realized that they had made a grave mistake in supporting the

proposal for destruction. They all started crying together with Ishtar on their mistake. There was havoc for seven days and seven nights continuously. The huge boat of Utnapishtim wandered and tossed in the stormy winds on the rising flood waters. On the eighth day, the south wind that brought the flood slowed down and the turbulent waters began to calm down. The sun once again shone brightly and in its light the deities saw the scene of terrible destruction in full. Uttapishtim's boat became steady on the water and when the king was convinced that the raging storm was about to subside, he opened a window of the seventh floor and peeped out; The earth was completely submerged under a vast layer of flood waters. No signs of life were visible anywhere around. The living beings were only on his boat. As soon as the first ray of the sun fell on the king's face, he bowed down with reverence before the Sun, the beam of immense power. He bowed down to Surya and other gods. Among the animals that he had given shelter on his boat, he sacrificed a bull and a sheep to the gods. Utnapishtim is deeply saddened by the sight of the complete destruction of life on earthWent and started crying sitting. In the water spread all around, he could not know where he was at that time. The peaks of all the mountains were completely submerged in water. He closed the window and let the boat float on the water for the next twelve days. On the twelfth day he opened the window, then he saw that his boat was stuck on the top of Mount Nisir. For the next seven days the boat stood there, as if tied to the top of a mountain. On the seventh day, the king made a pigeon fly in the sky. The pigeon kept flying for a while but when it did not see any other place to sit and rest, it returned to the boat. After some time, Utnapishtim offered food and drink to the gods on the top of Mount Nisir. Attracted by the smell of the offering, all the deities immediately gathered around the king. The king prostrated before the gods Anu and Enlil. Goddess Ishtar was very pleased to see that the king had saved some of her creatures. She mourned the dead and cursed Enlil for the destruction he had done. On the contrary, Enlil was enraged to see that the king and the other beings were safe inside the boat. He immediately asked the gods, "Which one of you allowed the king and all those on the boat to escape?"
Annoyance came that when he had given a clear order that not even a single sign of life should remain on earth in the holocaust, then how did Utnapishtim and the creatures

and substances on his boat survive? Eya stepped forward when Enlil was incensed and told Enlil that the purpose of the flood was to punish sinners and criminals, but punishment does not mean indiscriminate total destruction. Eya also told Enlil that he was not responsible for Utnapishtim's escape. He said that "Utnapishtim had seen a dream in which he was warned of the danger of the cataclysm and was also told how to avoid it and live." The soul must have been pure, that's why he had such a dream and he escaped from the horrifying holocaust. So he took the hand of the king and his wife and took them to the boat and blessed them. Enlil granted him immortality and praised him for providing protection to mankind, animals and plant seeds. Enlil allowed Utnapishtim to re-establish his kingdom in Shurappaka and told him to "reset the humans you protected on your boat in Shurappaka and restore life to this earth." Do it." Hearing this, Utnapishtim prayed to the gods.

bowed down to Due to a just and generous king who loved his land and subjects, life once again returned to the earth.

Myths of India

The origin of human –

beings In the Indian myths, the Trimurti Brahma, Vishnu, Mahesh have been given a prominent place, in which Vishnu is considered as the Adi Purush. The first form that the formless Brahma took was called Vishnu, who by the power of his will gave birth to Prajapati for the creation of the universe. Before the creation of the universe, Brahman was spread in the entire space. Till then he neither had any form nor name. Don't know how there was a stir in Brahma and Brahma felt - "I am one, I will become many." Water is called Nara in Sanskrit language because it originated from Brahma i.e. Nara. Brahm assumed the form and made water i.e. Nar as his house i.e. Ayan. That's why his name was Narayan. Due to the entry of Narayan's power in that Naar i.e. water, a huge golden egg appeared. After residing in that egg for one year, Hiranyagarbha i.e. Brahma was born. The same thing was told in another way that Narayan was sleeping passively on the bed of Sheshnag in the water, as the creation of the universe was taking place within him., As soon as the feeling came, the quality of passion was generated in his mind. This Rajogun suddenly rose up from his navel in the form of a lotus cord, on which a lotus flower blossomed, from which Brahma was born. After coming out of the golden egg, Hiranyagarbha Brahma broke it into two pieces. From one piece he made the sky and from the other piece the earth was established on water. Brahma produced sons with his will and asked them to create the universe, but they were not interested in this work. Seeing this, Brahma got angry and from the middle of his eyebrows, a child named Neelalohit i.e. blue and red was born. This child started crying as soon as it was born. Hence Brahma called it Rudra. It was Rudra who became the ancestor of the deities. After giving eleven names and forms to Rudra, Brahma gave him eleven wives, who were called Rudranis. The progeny that Rudra produced out of anger was also fiercely angry and started destroying the creation created by Brahma. Then Brahma told Rudra that now you should stop producing children and do penance. After this, Brahma created Narada from the lap, Daksha from the thumb, Vasistha from life, skin Bhrigu, Krit from hand, Pulah from navel, Pulastya from ears, Angira from mouth, Atri from eyes and Marichi from mind. Apart from religion, unrighteousness, work, anger, greed, among the other children of Brahma, there was Saraswati, the goddess of knowledge and speech. saraswati veryShe was a beautiful and pure minded girl, yet seeing her, desire arose in Brahma's mind. Saraswati explained to the father, due to which guilt arose in Brahma's mind and he left that body. His body itself became darkness. After this he assumed another body but the sorrow remained in his mind that the universe was not expanding. He realized that without sex there would be no increase in the population. As soon as this thought came to his mind, Brahma became eager to create a woman, fear arose in his mind that if he created a woman, seeing her, his desire to get her himself could be awakened in the same way. , The way Saraswati was born and in that situation he would have to immerse his body once again. Therefore, by dividing his body into two parts, he thought it more appropriate to create man and woman. As soon as this resolution came in his mind, his body automatically got divided into two parts. A part of Brahma's body became a man. He was called Manu. The second part became a woman, which was called Shatrupa. Manu took Shatrupa as his wife. Overall, there was no significant difference in the situation this time also. Manu was actually Brahma. In this way, the woman whom Brahma created from his own part had to take the form of Manu and accept her as his wife, there was no other solution.

The only difference remained that the mind was not a complete Brahma but a part of Brahma and Shatrupa was another part, while Saraswati was the daughter of Brahma and an independent goddess. From the time of Brahma's dismemberment and the emergence of Manu and Shatrupa, the wife is called the husband's half wife. Manu and Shatrupa were the first human (male) and the first human (female) to appear on this earth. Both of them were Swayambhu, that is, they were not born from the womb of any mother. Manu and Shatrupa produced five children through sexual intercourse, two sons named Priyavrata and Uttanpad and three daughters named Aakriti, Devhuti and Prasuti. These five children were the first human beings to be born on this earth from the womb of the mother staying in the womb with the help of the father. Manu married his three daughters to the three sons of Brahma, Ruchi Prajapati, Maharishi Kardama and Daksha Prajapati, respectively. Manu's son Priyavrat was married to the daughter of Vishwakarma Prajapati and Uttanpad was married to two god girls named Suruchi and Suniti. Dhruv, the son of Uttanpad, was very ascetic and . Became godly. Thus Manu and Shatrupa are the progenitors of the entire human race. Every human being is his descendant, whether he is fair, pale, wheatish or black, male or female, high caste or low caste, rich or poor or East or West. This also proves that man himself is the creator.

It is a part of existence itself and is not different from it in any way. That is why it has been said that God has created man in the form of his own shadow.

Greek myth

The creator of mankind –

The emperor of the immortal gods and his father Zeus is also the creator of mankind. Zeus is said to have given birth to five generations of humans, symbolizing the five yugas or five stages of human civilization – the Golden Age, the Silver Age, the Bronze Age, the Heroic Age and the Iron Age. The Golden Generation originated in the golden age of human civilization. The highest human values and virtues were naturally present in him. That generation was self-disciplined and it neither needed law, nor police, nor court. At that time there was a kingdom of peace everywhere on the earth. Human life was considered the highest value and mankind was completely free from greed, hatred, slavery and any kind of pain and suffering. It was an era of divine grace and prosperity. In this era, rivers of milk and nectar used to flow on the earth and honey flowed automatically from the trees. The pastures were green and milch cattle and sheep were in plenty. At that time man did not have the tendency to collect. Neither did he build forts, army or weapons for protection. the whole human race was free from diseasesAnd men left the body peacefully, as if death were a state of blissful and eternal sleep. After the passing of this golden age or golden age, Zeus created the silver generation of human beings. This was the second generation.

In this second age, the purity and sanctity of man's mind was destroyed and he became quarrelsome. This enraged Zeus and he ended the twelve months of spring on earth to punish the Silver Generation. On his order the year was divided into four seasons. In this era, man started building houses for his living and started growing perfumes by plowing the fields with the help of oxen. Zeus reduced the life span of humans and after death ordered their souls to be sent to Hades. This was the era in which man first experienced lack, suffering, pain and struggle. The third generation produced by Zeus was the Bronze Generation. After the rise of this generation, an era of war, violence, destruction and cruelty descended on the earth and human civilization moved towards its downfall. Then Zeus created a better generation than him. This was the heroic generation, which was more virtuous and better than the people of the silver and bronze generations. This heroic generation is high throughout lifeFighting for the cause. Zeus blessed the heroic generation with eternal life, peace and bliss. Eventually Zeus produced the fifth generation of humans. This is the iron generation, the present generation. According to the myth, the Iron Age would be an age of darkness, in which human life would be full of sorrow. Will be afflicted by grief, envy, strife, disease, death, crime, violence, greed and injustice. The Iron generation will be greedy and hoarding. Whatever Mother Earth produces, she will not be satisfied with that much and will rip open her stomach and exploit the wealth hidden in her womb. She will invade space and loot other planets to get their wealth. According to the myth, the Iron Generation is the last generation of the creation of Zeus. Which we call Kaliyuga in Indian myth. This generation is destined to be engaged in suicidal wars. The myth predicts for this age that there will be neither love nor respect between parents and children and there will be a conflict of interests between the two. The children will not care for their parents and elders when they become old and virtuous people will not be given any importance in this era. The present inhabitants of the earth are the humans of this iron generation. The part of the myth of Zeus that is related to this generation. That part gets 100% correct. The myth says that one day Zeus will feel that the Iron Generation will destroy all generations of his offspring.

I am the most unfit and useless, so that generation has no right to live on the earth and then it will destroy it. Perhaps this time Zeus will not have to exert himself at all to destroy the human race. We ourselves are so foolish that we will completely destroy our generation i.e. the present human race. The dark clouds of ego and love of materialism have completely covered the divine light and intelligence within us. We are devoting all our energies to the creation of the means of destruction to create a mass catastrophe on this earth and other planets and the complete destruction of the human race is almost certain. Perhaps this time Zeus himself has made us the means of our destruction.

Myths of Japan

Japan is an ancient country. It is very rich in terms of myths. According to the myths of creation, Japan, in the beginning this world was a crude oily ocean. Before the creation of the world, a reed-like substance emerged from it. This was the first deity. At that time neither the sky nor the earth was created. Gradually, the lighter element of the oily metropolis became sky and the denser and heavier part became earth. In the beginning the earth was just a heap of mud andThere was no gravitational force, so the earth used to float in the void between the sky and the oily sea. The first god Narakula also floated in a state of weightlessness. Along with Narkul Devta, two other deities also emerged, about whom in Japanese myths only mention is found in the rainbow that many generations of deities were born from their union. The first two deities to be mentioned in Japanese mythology are Izanagi and Izanami. In these, Aizanagi is the male element and Aizanami Prakriti or female element. They were born in heaven i.e. Devlok and passed through the moment to the bottom of the oily ocean - . had reached near. They were brother and sister to each other. The brother asked the sister, "Do you see the solid earth below?" To this Izanami replied that she could see nothing but liquid all around. I should take a spear encrusted with the jewel of heaven and bury it in the ocean to find out whether there is any dense or solid substance there. If it is there, it will automatically be known when the spear is buried. Both Aizanagi and Aizanami put the spear together in their Held it in his hands and dipped it in the ocean of oil, the land could not be detected with the spear, but when he took it out of the sea, it was stuck to the spear which was oily.

The material fell to the bottom of the ocean, solidified to form a mud-like substance, which Izanagi and Izanami collected to form the first landmass, Ono Koro Island. After the formation of the island on the ocean floor, Izanagi and Izanami landed on this island from the rainbow. He built a beautiful palace on the island and placed the Spear of Heaven as the main pillar in the center of the palace. Now both of them - - got married to each other. Despite becoming husband and wife, they were unaware of the process of male-female cohabitation. One day both of them were standing on the sea shore that suddenly their vision went on a pair of birds engrossed in intercourse. That scene created a feeling of coitus in his heart and taught him the art of night work. After that she gave birth to eight beautiful children, each of whom took the form of an island. The country of Japan is made up of these eight islands. After the land was created, Izanagi and Izanami gave birth to the gods of wind, mountain, valley, forest, stream, green fields and trees. After this, on the request of Aizanagi, Aizanami produced Amateras, the ruler of the world and the goddess of the sun.

The Maya Myth of Mexico:

The Creation of Man –

A rich ancient civilization, called the Maya civilization, arose in Guatemala in Central America and the Yucatan Peninsula of Mexico in the Middle Ages. It started 6,000 years before Christ and in 1524 AD the Spaniards who came from Europe completely destroyed that civilization. Maya civilization has been very rich in terms of myths. The Maya people were great astronomers and they built temples on huge and very high square pyramids for the worship of their gods. They were basically sun worshipers. Chaak, the god of rain, is counted among their main deities, to please whom the people of Maya civilization used to sacrifice virgin girls inside a well. That well is in the precincts of the Chichen Itza Temple in Yucatan. The gods of Maya civilization also wanted to create human beings like the gods of other civilizations. How they achieved this goal and what kind of humans they wanted to create, this thing is well expressed in their myths. Rise of the Earth In the beginning of creation there was neither wind nor fire, there was peace and silence all around. The whole earth was covered with a vast layer of water and the sky was spread over it. The third one was nothing. Till that time life was not created in the universe but the existence of gods- Was . The deities covered with green and blue feathers lived under the layer of water. He was very intelligent. Once they discussed two questions together. The first question was that how to remove the earth from the bottom of the water and the second was that how to remove the darkness prevailing all around? After a long discussion, one day the deities resolved to create the universe. They set before themselves some immediate goals: to fill the void, to limit the ocean in such a way that the earth can rise and the light can be created. The deities together prayed to the earth to rise up and fulfill their wishes. The earth accepted his prayer. She started rising and the sea started retreating. Mountains arose on the earth and beautiful forests grew in the rich soil of the mountains. After some time the second assembly of the deities took place. In which he expressed satisfaction over the rise of earth, mountains and forests and declared them as his masterpiece. Now the basic question before them was whether they should allow the silence and silence spread all around or create life under the trees on the hills and in the swamps of the plains, so that there could be movement in the creation. Finally, with the determination to break the silence of the universe, he first created birds, animals and snakes. The gods have given these living beings different places to rest, move around and make nests.

Gave place He also provided them with speech and told them to "raise your voices." asked for. But birds, animals and snakes could not sing in praise of the gods because their sounds were not clear.

Seeing the <u>creation of human</u> beings, the gods decided to create such a superior race of living beings, which would rule over animals, birds and snakes and kill them for food. The gods hoped that the creatures of that new race would be able to give them enough love and appreciation. Ultimately, they created new types of creatures from clay, but the samples made from clay were not satisfactory because on the one hand, due to the softness of the clay, those creatures could not bear the shocks of nature, on the other hand, their language was similar to that of the gods. Did not understand and thirdly they could not develop the ability to produce children. The deities destroyed those samples and made a new one out of wood. The specimen was hard and strong like wood and the new creatures resembled humans in terms of appearance and sound. The gods liked that specimen and created that breed.

Started it, but the biggest fault remained in them that their faces became completely emotionless. They had no soul, no blood, and no love for the gods who created them. Eventually the deities wanted to destroy those wooden samples too but it was as easy as destroying the clay samples. The wooden creatures opposed the gods and most of them were killed, those who survived had their faces scorched so badly that their progeny became monkeys. The deities were in search of a new material from which they could create human beings according to their imagination. One day four animals of the forest came to the gods and invited the gods to go with them. He took them to a place where yellow and white ears of corn stood in abundance. The deities took out grain from those earrings, ground it and created four superior beings from its flour. Gods prepared food and drinks from grains and fed them to humans in the form of food. The result of this was that those human beings of the sample started developing in terms of strength and intelligence. Now the deities declared that they were satisfied with the human beings created from grains. He called that human race his best creation. Those samples of human beings had to pass through the phase of examination. The gods wanted to see how these four human beings, the model they had created and whom they liked,

Whether or not they express their appreciation and love towards them. Those four ancestors of mankind were very intelligent and clever. He had the power to understand all the secrets of the universe. He was able to know the secrets of the sky and the earth beyond mountains and valleys, rivers and oceans. Knowing those mysteries, he was amazed and his heart was filled with a storm of admiration and love for the gods who created the universe. He thanked the gods for his creation and expressed his gratitude to them for seeing, hearing, speaking, thinking, feeling and moving and for the power to discriminate between good and bad and right and wrong. The gods were very pleased to see those four human beings in the sample expressing gratitude, love and appreciation towards them, but a doubt arose in their mind that the human beings in the sample might have become as knowledgeable and elevated as the gods. Unable to tolerate this, he misted the eyes of the four men in the sample, limiting their sharpness and far-sightedness. Now the gods gave their final approval to the four humans of the sample and created a woman for each of them. When he woke up from sleep and saw his wives beside him, he became even more grateful to the gods. Now the creation of the world started in full swing. God on the one handMore and more humans were engaged in forming pairs, on the other hand pairs of humans were producing children. They lived in the country part. Some of them were fair and some were black, some were rich and some were poor, but all the people kept praying to the gods for children and light.

Reference - World Famous Myths and Mythology.

Language

To express his thoughts, man first used language in whatever form it may be, then started using script to keep it safe.

Definition of language– A whole book can be written on this subject, but here in brief some definitions have been given. The meaning of language is to express ideas. Ideas can be expressed in many ways. Arm gestures, mouth gestures, finger and hand gestures (scouts are still taught to talk like deaf-dumbs with finger gestures) and pronunciation of sound, all these means are forms of language. But in the present era Expressing thoughts only by speaking is called 'language'. Language is the result of mental action. Thought is the life or soul of language. Language is the external and physical form of those thoughts. Language is the sum of all those signs that we have. Regenerate thoughts by taking in emotions and other external thoughts and can repeat them again if necessary.

The movement of the vocal cords is not language, but it is the external environment that forces the vocal cords to move, that is, whatever a person imbibes in the subconscious mind, it is language that reproduces. Language is accepted by everyone but not created by everyone. Man's heart and mind are a mint, in which first of all uncontemplated feelings, thoughts appear as a reaction of heart and mind. Thinking of unconscious is the first stage of language. When random thoughts become the subject of contemplation, then the second stage begins. The first stage is the basis of the second stage. It is the embodiment of the abstract and the personification of the unmanifested. This is the ladder where language is born.

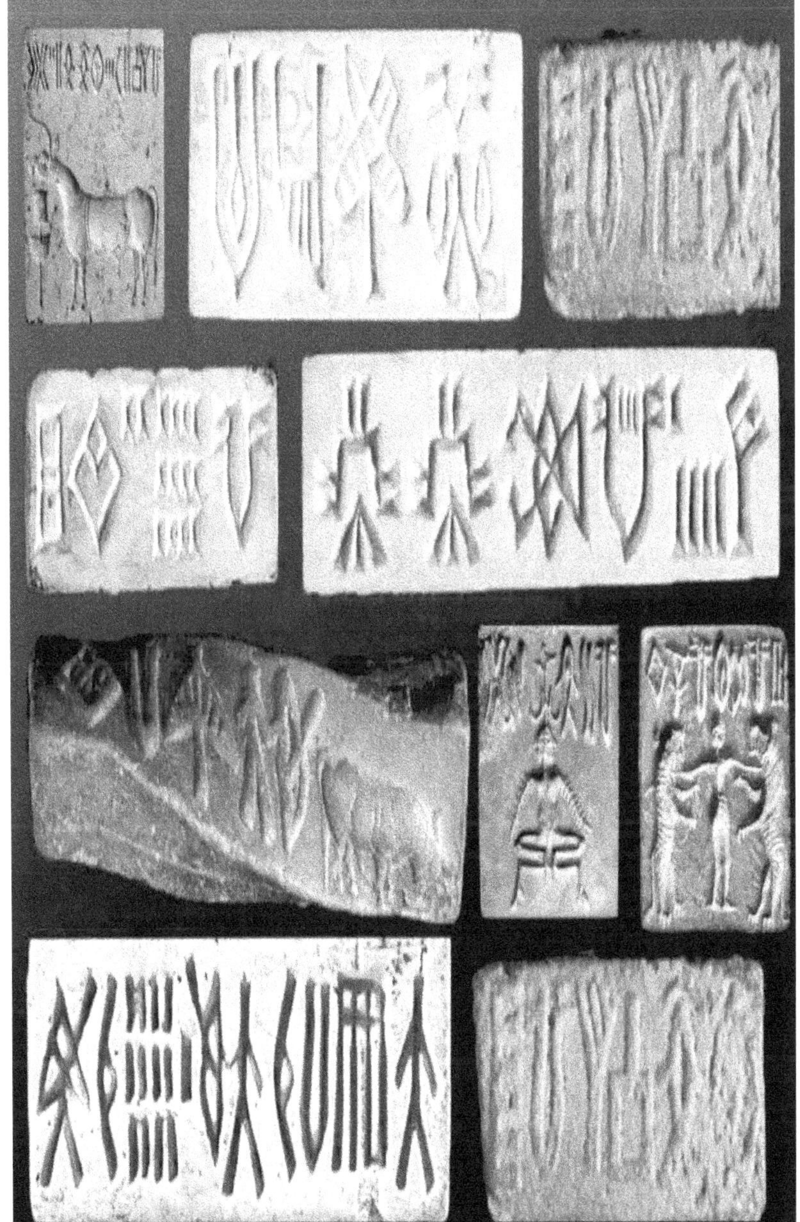

Words and sentences have to be tied in some method to make the language meaningful. The words have to be uttered according to the prescribed rules. These words themselves are made by extracting continuous sounds from special places and these sounds are made differently by the touch of different tongues. The form changes when the sounds come out of the nose. Sometimes we reach a sound that we cannot break down any more. Letters are made by imagining such sounds. The quality of a scientific language is that the letters to be written should not represent more than one sound, nor any one. There should be such a letter that it can be written but it cannot be pronounced. Language is a coin minted in the mint of the mind which, passing through unthought lines, is shaped by the object of concern. One more thing is worth noting. Ideas are expressed through sentences. A sentence is the smallest component of a language. The smallest external form of our thought is a sentence, not words, but words are made by adding words. Thoughts have feelings. Similarly, there are words within a sentence. Just as thought comes before emotion, in the same way a sentence comes before a word. Just as there is no state of a separate feeling, similarly there is no existence of a word independent of the sentence. Therefore the ultimate component of language is the sentence, not the word or letter.

Nabatean	Name	Arabic Alphabet	Syriac Alphabet	Nabatean	Name	Arabic Alphabet	Syriac Alphabet
	Alaph	ا			Lamadh	ل	
	Beth	ب			Meem	م	
	Gamal	ج			Noon	ن	
	Dalath	د			Simkath	س	
	Heh	ه			E	ع	
	Waw	و			Peh	ف	
	Zain	ز			Sad'e	ص	
	Heth	ح			Qoph	ق	
	Teth	ط			Resh	ر	
	Yodh	ى			Sheen	ش	
	Kaph	ك			Taw	ت	

Origin of language.

1 Language is now not only a language, but has become a linguistic science and great scientific research has been done on it and will continue to happen in the future. Language originated millions of years ago, to find out when and how it Started, not enough base available. In such a situation only guesswork can be resorted to. Because imagination or conjecture cannot come under science, this Because the subject of the origin of language cannot be considered a part of the subject of linguistics. Keeping this idea in mind, when the Council of Linguistics (La Societe de Linguistique) was established in Paris in 1866, the founders banned the consideration of the origin of language.   Nevertheless, the human nature of bringing the unknowable into the purview of the Sheya forced the scholars to think about the origin, whose conclusions are as follows:

1.   All the ancient countries were God-oriented by the gods; in the absence of knowledge, everything which was unknowable to the immediate man, was done for the sake of God. On this principle, the origin of language was also done for the sake of God. Panini's 14 sutras originated from the sound of Shiva's drum. Sanskrit was considered to be the language of God, Arabic to Allah and Hebrew to Jehovah. This ancient idea is equally strong even today that a child learns language by listening only after birth, that is why the deaf cannot speak. -

2. By imitation man heard the sounds of animals and birds in his environment and words were made for the sounds. For example, mo bhi for barking dog, 7 for horse. To exhale, 'whining', lion's roar, elephant's squeal etc.

In the same way, 'Sanyan Sanyan' by the wind, 'thak thak' by the beating of wood, crackling by lightning (of the sky) etc.

3. Through impulse (pooh-pooh theory) to express anger, love, puna etc. some sounds are used accidentally, like prad, oh, chhih etc. 4. Through labour: (after ho ho): When a man does physical labor, then naturally some kind of sounds come out from the throat, such as 'Chhio Chhio' of the washerman, 'Hey ho' of the boatman etc.

5. Aadhaar is also an imitation of this by means of signs, but not of external things, but of the parts of one's own body, which should not be done knowingly, but should be done by oneself (Unconscious imitation). , -

6. Man is a social animal through contact. In the early days, when man used to live in groups in the forests, he used to eat tubers, roots, fruits, etc., whatever circumstances he came in contact with, he used to force himself to eat tubers, roots, fruits, etc. For example, if he saw a lion or a bear, he made the sound of do do or to to to. slowly slowly this sound as a signal to the people of that groupHas been determined. In the same way, the symbolic sounds kept on increasing and with the human development, the development of sounds continued. The main reason for this development was connectivity:

7. Agreed theory When those groups came in contact with other groups which brought other types of sounds with them, new meditations were born by their combination and in this way some gestures, some imitation, some expressions, some due to external environment change with sounds. Sentences became words and words became letters. This work was completed in millions of years.

Spread of language

Some people lived in one region for centuries, similarly some others lived in another region. When the food there ran out, some went to new places. The dialect of those places was different. For this reason it was natural for the language to be hybrid; Today 27 9 63 would have been made through which a new language was born. Languages made in this way have become and it is possible that some more may become.

Valeur (Syriaque)	Valeur (Samaritain)	Valeur (Arabe)	Valeur (Arabe suite)
A	H	A	L
B	S	B	M
C	V	Ts	N
D	H	Dj	U
E	D	H	V
F	G	Kh	Y
Z	B	D	
H	A	Dz	
Th (grec)	E	R	
I	Ç	Z	
K	N	Sç	
L	M	Chsch	
M	L	Sc	
N	K	Dh	
Cse grec	I	Th	
O	T	Dh	
P	Th	H	
Ts	Sch	G	
Q	R	F	
R	Q	K	
S	Tz	Oc	
T	P		

Dialect and Language

There is a lot of difference between dialect and language, but even many educated people do not understand. The range of speech is narrow while the range of language is wide, but earlier there was no limit of wideness. With the birth of nationalism, the limit of universality was bounded with the boundary of the country and the nation became the national language by joining the language. To understand their difference, linguists have determined three forms, which are as follows:

1. Individual dialect (Idiolect) is the shortest form of individual spoken language. There is a difference in the language of a person from his birth till his death, which is quite visible. Children call water mum, food Happu or Pappu etc. and they change as they grow up. ,

2. Local Dialect It is a collective form of many individual dialects. There is no difference between them.

3. **Language**: It is a collective form of many local dialects. in this . There is definitely some difference between each other. The provinces of India were created on the basis of regional languages, but many dialects are prevalent in one province.

vowels and consonants in language— Their definition is necessary. This book will prove to be helpful in understanding the scripts. The definition of vowels and consonants is as follows: [1] 7 **Vowels**: Those letters of a language can be heard from a distance, can be spoken for a long time without any help, some Be able to speak with open mouth etc. The basic vowels are: -B - I U Wh ' The rest of the vowels are made of their combination. Consonants: They are letters that can be heard close to vowels. The distance of the sound will be left.

Differences in the languages of the world

The First World War ended in 1988 and the countries became independent. Man became dependent, his freedom to come and go was banned, the contacts started decreasing. National-languages started becoming bigotry, then changes in languages also became difficult. Now the difficulty that is in front is that if a person wants to pronounce the letters of a country correctly, it is impossible because one letter or alphabet is 'G' of Roman; Somewhere it has the sound 'g' and somewhere 'j'. Similarly 'C' is, somewhere it gives the pronunciation of 'S' and somewhere the language of 'K' can be learned only when it remains among those people whose language it is. Many efforts have been made in this direction that human Unity of language is necessary for unity, but due to the bigotry of nationalism and other difficulties, the efforts could not be successful.

My another books

Sr no.	Book
1	World's Major religions, doctrines and sects
2	An introduction to the Holy Qur'an and it's unsolved mysteries
3	How did humans and language originate ?
4	Islam an introduction and sect
5	Sermons of great people
6	Prayer
7	Allah an introduction
8	Is Al khizr still alive today?
9	Story of harut and marut
10	Grief
11	The mysterious story of Al kahf (Ar raqim)
12	Naming of God

All these books are available in Hindi language and other international languages and are also available in e-book for free on Google Play Store.

My personal introduction

My name is Abdul Waheed, my father's name is Late Haji Ubaidur Rahman and mother's name is Jaibunnisa. I have liked scientific ideology since childhood and have a calm nature and attachment to books. Due to which my curiosity interest has been continuously used in new discoveries and information. I got selected in polytechnic while doing BSc, but unfortunately it remained incomplete because father and brother died.

Two words of my father, which are very precious for my life,

first - earn honestly, do not take support of lies,

secondly, respect food and eat as much as you want. That's why the education remained incomplete due to the responsibility of the house, then later getting married. Still did not lose courage and today the book is available in front of you in the form of my thoughts. If any information is left incomplete, please let us know. ,

Thank you .

Contact-

yours– Abdul Waheed, Barabanki, UP, India.

https://www.facebook.com/profile.php?id=100091298026218